BABY-SITTERS LITTLE SISTER
SUMMER FILL-IN

THIS BOOK BELONGS TO

Look for these and other books about Karen in the Baby-sitters Little Sister series:

#1 Karen's Witch
#2 Karen's Roller Skates
#3 Karen's Worst Day
#4 Karen's Kittycat Club
#5 Karen's School Picture
#6 Karen's Little Sister
#7 Karen's Birthday
#8 Karen's Haircut
#9 Karen's Sleepover
#10 Karen's Grandmothers
#11 Karen's Prize
#12 Karen's Ghost
#13 Karen's Surprise
#14 Karen's New Year
#15 Karen's in Love
#16 Karen's Goldfish
#17 Karen's Brothers
#18 Karen's Home Run
#19 Karen's Good-bye
#20 Karen's Carnival
#21 Karen's New Teacher
#22 Karen's Little Witch
#23 Karen's Doll
#24 Karen's School Trip
#25 Karen's Pen Pal
#26 Karen's Ducklings
#27 Karen's Big Joke
#28 Karen's Tea Party
#29 Karen's Cartwheel
#30 Karen's Kittens
#31 Karen's Bully
#32 Karen's Pumpkin Patch
#33 Karen's Secret
#34 Karen's Snow Day
#35 Karen's Doll Hospital
#36 Karen's New Friend
#37 Karen's Tuba

#38 Karen's Big Lie
#39 Karen's Wedding
#40 Karen's Newspaper
#41 Karen's School
#42 Karen's Pizza Party
#43 Karen's Toothache
#44 Karen's Big Weekend
#45 Karen's Twin
#46 Karen's Baby-sitter
#47 Karen's Kite
#48 Karen's Two Families
#49 Karen's Stepmother
#50 Karen's Lucky Penny
#51 Karen's Big Top
#52 Karen's Mermaid
#53 Karen's School Bus
#54 Karen's Candy
#55 Karen's Magician
#56 Karen's Ice Skates
#57 Karen's School Mystery
#58 Karen's Ski Trip
#59 Karen's Leprechaun
#60 Karen's Pony
#61 Karen's Tattletale
#62 Karen's New Bike
#63 Karen's Movie
#64 Karen's Lemonade Stand

Super Specials:

#1 Karen's Wish
#2 Karen's Plane Trip
#3 Karen's Mystery
#4 Karen, Hannie, and Nancy: The Three Musketeers
#5 Karen's Baby
#6 Karen's Campout

BABY-SITTERS LITTLE SISTER
SUMMER FILL-IN

Ann M. Martin

A
LITTLE APPLE
PAPERBACK

SCHOLASTIC INC.
New York Toronto London Auckland Sydney

*The author gratefully acknowledges
Julie Komorn
for her help
with this book.*

Cover art by Susan Tang
Interior art by John DeVore

ISBN 0-590-26467-2

Copyright © 1995 by Ann M. Martin.
All rights reserved. Published by Scholastic Inc.
BABY-SITTERS LITTLE SISTER and APPLE PAPERBACKS are registered trademarks of Scholastic Inc.

12 11 10 9 8 7 6 5 4 3 2 1   5 6 7 8 9/9 0/0

Printed in the U.S.A.   40

First Scholastic printing, June 1995

HURRAY FOR SUMMER!

These are some of the things the Three Musketeers wanted to do over summer vacation: ride our bikes, roller skate, go to the playground, swim, do arts and crafts, and read, read, READ!

FROM SUPER SPECIAL #4 KAREN, HANNIE, AND NANCY: THE THREE MUSKETEERS

Hurray! No more school or homework. Summer has finally arrived! And there are so many fun things to do. Karen is very excited about summer. Are you?

Here is your chance to remember every fun moment of summer. All you have to do is fill in the details — so grab your pen or pencil and get started. Along the way you can paste in photos, draw pictures, and collect autographs. When you are finished you will have a book filled with your very own special summer memories.

Here is a picture of me at the beginning of summer.

Draw a picture or paste a photograph of yourself here.

This picture is of me

on _____ (date)

at _____ (place).

ALL ABOUT ME!

I am Karen Brewer. I am seven years old. I wear glasses. I have freckles and blonde hair and blue eyes. This is my nickname: Blarin' Karen.

FROM #37 KAREN'S TUBA

My name is Ashley Marie Buchanan

My nickname is Shortey.

I am 11 years old.

The color of my hair is Brownish-Blonde

The color of my eyes is Blue.

I ☐ do ☒ do not wear glasses.

I am 4 feet 6 inches tall.

I weigh 70 pounds.

My address is 102 Cedar St
Smithville, MO. 64089
.

My phone number is (816)-532-3746.

LAST DAY OF SCHOOL

I banged through the front door of Mommy's house. I banged into the kitchen. I dropped my things all over the floor — pencils, papers, an old workbook, three flower erasers, two sticks of gum, a papier-mâché rabbit, and a folder full of paintings.

It was the last day of school.

I had cleaned out my desk.

FROM SUPER SPECIAL #4 KAREN, HANNIE, AND NANCY: THE THREE MUSKETEERS

STONEYBROOK ELEMENTARY

The last day of school was on ___May 30th___.

The name of my school is ___Smithville Elm___.

I was in ___5th___ grade.

My teacher's name was ___Mrs. Yolma Jensen___

On the last day of school we _____

_____.

The thing about school that I am really going to miss is

_____

_____.

The funniest thing that happened at school last year was

_____

_____

_____

_____

_____

_____

_____

_____

_____

_____

_____

_____

_____.

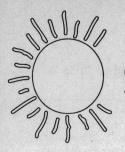

SUMMER BUDDIES

Hannie and Nancy and I call ourselves the Three Musketeers. We are going to be best friends forever and for always. I had big summer plans for my friends and me. We were going to stay together as much as possible.

FROM SUPER SPECIAL #4 KAREN, HANNIE, AND NANCY: THE THREE MUSKETEERS

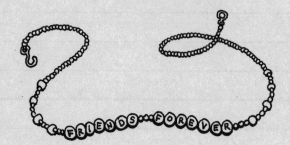

These are the names of my best friends: _____

_____.

My silliest friend is _____.

My most athletic friend is _____.

My most artistic friend is _____.

Sometimes Karen and her friends like to play Lovely Ladies. When I am with my friends we like to _____

_____.

Our favorite place to hang out is _____

_____.

The friend I can tell my secrets to is _____

_____.

The friend that I have known the longest is _____

_____.

We've known each other since _____.

A new friend that I made this summer was _____

_____.

I met my new friend at _____

_____.

The best thing I did with my new summer friend was___

_____

_____

_____

_____

_____

_____.

FRIENDS FOREVER

Here is a picture of my summer friend(s) and me:

**Draw a picture or paste in a photograph of you
and a friend or friends.**

This is a picture of me and _____ .

Date:_____

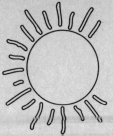

MY FAMILY

Do you want to know the most interesting thing of all about me? I have two *families. That's because a long time ago, my mommy and daddy got divorced. Then they each got married again. Mommy married Seth. He is my stepfather. Daddy married Elizabeth. She is my stepmother.*

FROM #6 KAREN'S LITTLE SISTER

I have _____ people in my family.

My family's names and ages: _____

_____

_____.

I am the ☐ oldest ☐ middle
        ☐ youngest ☐ only child.

The thing I like to do best with my family in the summer is _____.

Every summer my family _____.

The person in my family who likes summer the most is

_____.

SUMMER ANIMALS

"I know you probably won't let us do this."
. . . "What do you want to do?" asked Daddy.

"Get a pet," I told him. "A pet for Andrew and me at the big house. Daddy, you have Boo-Boo, and David Michael has Shannon. And at Mommy's are Rocky and Midgie, but they belong to Seth. I have Emily Junior, but she has to stay at the little house. And poor, poor Andrew doesn't have any pet of his own."

FROM #16 KAREN'S GOLDFISH

I have ___ pet(s) named _____.

I got my pet(s) from _____.

I share my pet(s) with _____.

This is (These are) the age(s) of my pet(s): _____.

My favorite game to play with my pet(s) is _____.

My favorite place to take my pet is _____
_____.

If I could have any animal as a pet, I would like to have

_____.

I like my friend's pet named _____.

My favorite stuffed animal is named _____.

I have had it since _____.

**Paste or draw a picture of you and your pet
(or a pet you would like to have)
enjoying your favorite summer activity together.**

Date:_____

MEMORIAL DAY WEEKEND

I just love holidays. Like I said before, Memorial Day is not a huge holiday for either of my families. But when I woke up on Monday morning, I was gigundo excited. I checked outside. The sun was shining. No clouds!

FROM #18 KAREN'S HOME RUN

This is what I did on Memorial Day: _____

_____

_____.

The weather was _____.

I spent Memorial Day with _____.

The best part of the long weekend was _____

_____.

We ❑ did ❑ did not have a barbecue.

I know summer is going to be great because _____

_____.

SUMMER TRIPS

"Yea! Hurray! It is time to take," I sang, "all of my things to Shadow Lake!"

I was so happy. Our trip would begin the next day. I was in my room at the little house. I was packing my suitcase for the trip.

FROM SUPER SPECIAL #4 KAREN, HANNIE, AND NANCY: THE THREE MUSKETEERS

This summer I went on a vacation to _____
_____.

The people who went on the vacation were _____
_____
_____.

We left on _____ (date) and got back on _____ (date).

I ☐ overpacked ☐ underpacked ☐ packed perfectly.

The places we visited were _____
_____
_____.

The coolest thing I saw was _____
_____.

A souvenir I bought was _____
_____.

The funniest part of the trip was when _____
_____
_____.

☀ SUMMER TRAVELING

Andrew and I were sitting side by side in the backseat. The Fun Bags were between us. For awhile, we colored quietly. Then I drew some tic-tac-toe boards. Andrew and I played game after game, but I kept winning. . . .

"I know. Let's play the license plate game," I said.

Andrew and I gazed out our windows. We watched cars go by. . . .

"New York!" I called out.

"Maine!" Andrew called out.

"Arizona!"

FROM #52 KAREN'S MERMAID

This is how we got to our vacation spot:

❑ plane   ❑ train   ❑ car

❑ bus   ❑ boat   ❑ other

It took us _____ (hours / days) to get there.

A game I played while traveling was _____.

I ❑ never ❑ sometimes ❑ always feel sick
while I am traveling.

The best part of traveling is _____
_____.

Next year I hope to travel to _____
_____.

If I could go anywhere in the world, I would go to
_____

because _____
_____.

MY VACATION

Paste a souvenir, postcard,
or photograph from your vacation here.

Date:_____

SUMMER BIRTHDAYS

Saturday was my actual birthday. It was the day I would really turn seven. When I woke up on Saturday, the sun was shining and the sky was blue. It was perfect birthday weather!

At noon, my friends began arriving at the big house. "Happy birthday, Karen!" they cried.

FROM #7 KAREN'S BIRTHDAY

My birthday is on _____.

The best summer birthday party I ever went to was

_____.

I think the best thing to do at a summer birthday party
is _____.

I had my last birthday party at _____.

This is what we did: _____

_____.

The best gift I received was _____.

Here are the names of my friends and family who celebrate summer birthdays:

Name _____

    Birthday_____

Name_____

    Birthday_____

Name_____

    Birthday_____

Name_____

    Birthday_____

Name_____

    Birthday_____

Name_____

    Birthday_____

SUMMER PARTIES

"Hannie! Nancy!" I said in a loud whisper.
"What?" they answered.
"Daddy told me I could have a sleepover party!"

FROM #9 KAREN'S SLEEPOVER

My favorite summer party was at _____.

This is what we did: _____
_____.

My friend,_____ had
a pool party.

The weather was _____.

Here is an invitation I received to a summer party:
Paste your invitation here.

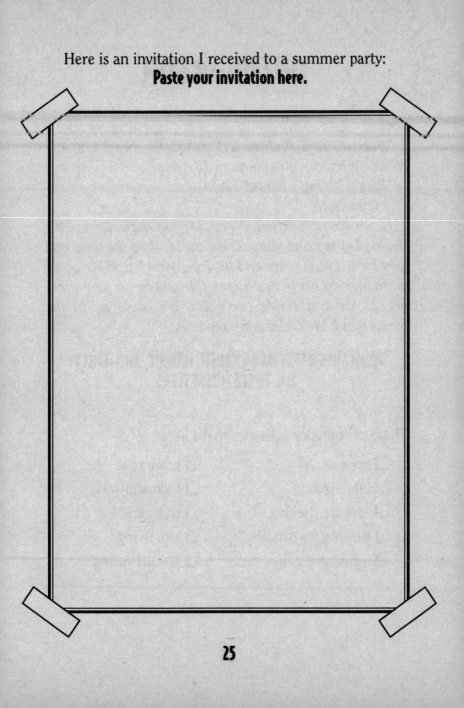

OUTDOOR FUN

"Karen?" said Andrew. He poked his head into my room. "What are you going to do today?". . .

"Play with my friends," I said.

"Play what?"

Hmm. Good question. We could do so many things. We could play tag and statues. We could sit in the yard and wait for the mail truck and the ice-cream truck. We could go to Melody Korman's house. (Melody has a swimming pool.) We could ride our bikes. We could go to the playground. We could paint pictures.

FROM SUPER SPECIAL #4 KAREN, HANNIE, AND NANCY: THE THREE MUSKETEERS

These are outdoor activities that I like:

- ❑ hopscotch
- ❑ bike riding
- ❑ capture the flag
- ❑ turning cartwheels
- ❑ miniature golf
- ❑ jump rope
- ❑ hide-and-seek
- ❑ tree climbing
- ❑ kite flying
- ❑ go-cart racing

On a hot day I like to cool off with these activities:

- ❑ having a water balloon toss
- ❑ sliding on a waterslide
- ❑ playing in the sprinkler
- ❑ relaxing under a shady tree
- ❑ splashing around in a kiddie pool
- ❑ riding my bike super-fast
- ❑ sipping a glass of ice cold lemonade

I ❑ did ❑ did not make a lemonade stand this summer.

I think a glass of lemonade should cost _____.

NEIGHBORHOOD FRIENDS

Hannie and Linny and I hung around on the Papadakises' driveway. After awhile, Andrew and David Michael came over. Then my friend Melody and her older brother Bill came over. Then Maria Kilbourne, who lives next door. Finally Timmy and Scott Hsu came over.

FROM #49 KAREN'S STEPMOTHER

The people who live next door to me are _____

_____

_____.

The people who live across from me are _____

_____

_____.

Friends who live down the block are _____

_____

_____.

We ❑ had ❑ did not have a block party this summer.

Some of the games I like to play with my friends on my block are _____

_____

_____.

I play with my neighborhood friends about _____ times a week.

SUMMER EATING

I have never seen so much food in my life. Except maybe at a grocery store. This is what was served at the picnic on Saturday — hamburgers, hot dogs, chicken, fruit salad, regular salad, deviled eggs, pie, and ice cream. The food was spread out on long tables.

FROM #38 KAREN'S BIG LIE

I ❑ like ❑ do not like picnics / cookouts.

The most fun I had at a picnic this summer was at

_____(place) on _____ (date).

These are the people who were there: _____

_____.

My favorite picnic food is _____.

If I could, I would eat it _____ times a week.

Other picnic foods I like to eat are:

❑ hot dogs   ❑ hamburgers
❑ chicken   ❑ s'mores
❑ lemonade   ❑ pickles
❑ chips   ❑ pie

- ❑ watermelon
- ❑ corn-on-the-cob
- ❑ regular salad
- ❑ ice cream
- ❑ macaroni / potato salad
- ❑ other _____

- ❑ bug juice
- ❑ fruit salad
- ❑ deviled eggs
- ❑ Popsicles
- ❑ soda

Some games we played at the picnic were

_____

_____.

The best thing that happened at the picnic was

_____

_____

_____.

ICE-CREAM FUN

"Hey! Nancy, do you hear that?"

"Hear what?"

"Listen. Bells. Mr. Tastee is coming!"

Mr. Tastee, the ice-cream man, cruises his truck slowly through the streets of our neighborhood in the summertime. When we run to the street he stops for us. Then we can buy Popsicles and ice-cream cones and ice-cream sandwiches.

FROM #50 KAREN'S LUCKY PENNY

My favorite ice-cream flavor is _____.

I prefer to eat my ice cream

☐ on a cone

☐ in a cup

These are some of the toppings that I like to put on my ice cream: _____

_____

We ☐ do ☐ do not have an ice-cream truck that drives through our neighborhood.

My favorite Popsicle flavor is _____.

Here is a picture of this summer's yummiest ice-cream:

SUMMER SWIMMING

Splash! Guess where I am. I am in Amanda Delaney's gigundo big swimming pool!

"I'm the Little Mermaid!" I said. "I am going to hunt for treasures!" I held my nose and —

"Wait. Who will I be?" asked Amanda.

"You can be my friend Flounder," I said. "Your job is to watch out for the . . . the shark! The shark is after us!" I shouted.

"Eeek!" yelled Amanda. We were yelling and giggling and racing around the pool.

FROM #19 KAREN'S GOOD-BYE

My favorite place to swim is _____.

I usually swim in
    ❏ a lake   ❏ a pool   ❏ the ocean
    ❏ a reservoir   ❏ a river   ❏ a pond
    ❏ other _____

The water is usually ❏ cold ❏ medium ❏ hot.

I usually do the
    ❏ breaststroke   ❏ backstroke   ❏ crawl
    ❏ sidestroke   ❏ butterfly

I think I am a ❏ fast ❏ pretty fast ❏ slow swimmer.

I like to
    ❏ jump   ❏ dive   ❏ flip
    ❏ cannonball   ❏ other _____ into the water.

I prefer
    ❏ the high dive   ❏ the low dive
    ❏ both   ❏ neither

I ❏ can ❏ cannot do flips underwater.

I ❏ do ❏ do not like to dive for pennies.

When I am in the water, I like to pretend I am

_____.

Games I like to play in the water are:_____

_____.

BEACH BUM

We were ready to play.

"Let's make sand castles!" called Margo when she saw me.

"No, let's go in the water," I said. So we did. We jumped over little waves. We looked for fish. We swam and splashed and shouted.

FROM #52 KAREN'S MERMAID

My favorite beach is _____.

Some things I like to take with me to the beach are:

❏ sunglasses   ❏ a towel

❏ snacks   ❏ a beach blanket

❏ suntan lotion   ❏ a radio

❏ cold drinks   ❏ a beach hat

❏ sunblock   ❏ lunch

❏ a beach chair   ❏ sandals

❏ flip-flops   ❏ a kite

❏ lip balm   ❏ a beach umbrella

❏ other _____

Beach games I like to play are: _____

_____.

Things I like to take in the water with me:

☐ inner tube   ☐ raft

☐ flippers   ☐ mask

☐ goggles   ☐ water toys

☐ a beach pail   ☐ a beachball

☐ other _____

The coolest thing I saw on the beach was _____.

The person I like to play in the water with is

_____.

I ☐ do ☐ do not like to bodysurf.

I ☐ do ☐ do not like to look for shells.

I ☐ do ☐ do not believe in mermaids.

I ☐ do ☐ do not like to look for fish.

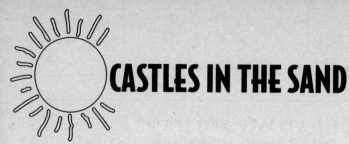

CASTLES IN THE SAND

I made a special dribble castle. I used dribbly wet sand from down by the water to decorate it. When it was finished, my castle looked like a birthday cake with icing dribbling down the sides. It was a wonderful fancy castle. I even built a drawbridge over the moat.

FROM #52 KAREN'S MERMAID

The best sand castle I made looked like _____
_____
_____.

The name of the beach where I made my castle was
_____.

I ❑ did ❑ did not build a moat around my castle.

The tools I used were _____

_____

_____.

I decorated my castle with _____

_____

_____.

These are the people who helped me with my castle:

_____

_____

_____

Other things I like to build out of sand are _____

_____

_____

_____

_____.

The person I like to bury in the sand most is

_____.

SPLASHING SPORTS

"Put on your cap, Karen Brewer," said Hank. "The race is about to start and we need you."

I stood at the edge of the dock. The whistle blew. Hannie flew into the water. I put my big toe in to see how cold it was. It was pretty cold, but everyone was yelling at me to jump. So I finally did.

FROM SUPER SPECIAL #6 KAREN'S CAMPOUT

I ❑ do ❑ do not like to swim relay races.

Other water sports that I enjoy are:

❑ boogie boarding	❑ skimboarding
❑ jet skiing	❑ surfing
❑ windsurfing	❑ waterskiing
❑ sailing	❑ canoeing
❑ rowboating	❑ kayaking
❑ snorkeling	❑ water polo
❑ fishing	

(I have caught _____ fish so far this summer.)

My favorite kind of boat is:

❑ sailboat	❑ canoe
❑ kayak	❑ pontoon
❑ speedboat	❑ raft
❑ yacht	❑ rowboat
❑ other _____	

SUMMER SPORTS

I was also nervous. Now the Krushers had two outs, and I was up at bat. I looked at the pitcher. I looked at the ball. I watched the ball as it came toward me.
THWACK! I hit the ball and ran to first base.

FROM #18 KAREN'S HOME RUN

My favorite sport is _____.

Other sports I enjoy in the summer are:

❑ tennis   ❑ baseball
❑ softball   ❑ soccer
❑ volleyball   ❑ gymnastics
❑ football   ❑ Frisbee
❑ lacrosse   ❑ archery
❑ hiking   ❑ basketball
❑ track   ❑ golf
❑ karate   ❑ field hockey
❑ relay races   ❑ running
❑ tug-of-war   ❑ horseback riding
❑ swimming

My greatest moment in sports was when I _____

_____.

My biggest sports blooper was when I _____

_____.

If I could choose anyone to be on my team, I would

choose _____.

The most exciting game I watched this summer was

between _____ and _____.

The final score was _____.

SUMMER CAMP

"Three days! Two days! One day! Fun day!"
That was my countdown-to-camp song. . . .
"It is summer vacation," I said. "In three more days I
will be going to Camp Mohawk."
. . . "I know everything there is to know about going to
camp. I know about horseback riding, swimming, and
hiking. I know about living in a cabin. I know about camp
food. And I know about having fun."

FROM SUPER SPECIAL #6 KAREN'S CAMPOUT

I went to Camp _____

in _____.

My counselor was _____.

The kids in my cabin were _____

_____

_____

_____

_____.

I learned to _____

_____

_____.

The best part of camp was _____

_____

_____.

The worst part of camp was _____

_____

_____.

One new friend I met at camp was _____.

The food at camp was _____.

I got an award or passed a test for _____.

My favorite campfire song is _____.

Here is a funny picture of me at camp:

SUMMER PEN PALS

"Karen, there's some mail here for you," called Mommy.

Hurray! Mail. That is one of the best things about going to camp. When you come home you get lots of letters from your camp friends.

FROM SUPER SPECIAL #6 KAREN'S CAMPOUT

I think getting mail is _____.

My favorite pen pal is _____.

I also look forward to getting letters from

_____.

The best news I got all summer was in a letter from

_____

that said _____

_____

_____.

The worst news I got all summer was in a letter from

_____

that said _____

_____

_____.

The funniest letter I got all summer was from

_____

who said _____

_____

_____.

I received the most letters from _____.

❏ I love to write letters.

❏ I hate to write letters.

❏ I think writing letters is okay.

So far I have written _____ letters this summer.

I sent the most letters to _____.

SUMMER MOVIES

Kristy sat behind us. My friends and I passed the popcorn back and forth. (We remembered to pass it to Kristy, too.) Soon the lights were turned out. A cartoon began. Then the feature came on. We had decided to see The Tale of the Bad Dog, *which sounded funny.*

When the movie ended, Hannie grinned at me. "That was great, Karen!"

FROM #50 KAREN'S LUCKY PENNY

My favorite movie this summer was_____.

The worst movie I saw was _____.

Some other movies I saw this summer were

_____

_____.

My favorite movie stars are _____

_____.

My favorite song from a movie is _____.

The person I like to go to the movies with most is _____

_____.

I like to munch on _____

_____

while I watch a movie.

If I wrote a movie, it would be about _____

_____

_____.

These are the people I would want to star in my movie:

_____

_____

SUMMER TV

Audrey pulled me inside. She led me into the TV room. A table had been set in front of the TV. (Well, not right in front of it, but near it.) She served us our lunch. Then she switched on The Little Mermaid.

I had seen that movie five or six times already. I love the story of Ariel. So I was happy to watch it again.

FROM #45 KAREN'S TWIN

I ❏ do ❏ do not like watching TV.

The TV show I like best is _____.

It is on _____ (day) at _____ (time)

on channel _____.

My favorite episode was when _____

_____.

My favorite TV star is _____.

If I could be the star of a TV show, I'd like to be _____

_____.

My favorite summer rerun was _____.

Other shows I like to watch are _____
_____
_____.

I can't wait to watch the new _____.
show this fall.

My favorite movie on TV is _____
_____.

I have watched it _____ times.

ARTS AND CRAFTS

I got out my collage. . . . I looked at what I had done so far. The paper was very full. But the collage was not quite right. I added some of the wood shavings I had found at Seth's workshop. Then I wrote some words on the paper. Did you know words can be part of a collage?

FROM #46 KAREN'S BABY-SITTER

The kinds of art I like to make or do are:

- ❏ collage
- ❏ painting
- ❏ tie-dying
- ❏ wood carving
- ❏ pottery
- ❏ clay
- ❏ lanyard
- ❏ macrame
- ❏ drawing
- ❏ ceramics
- ❏ batik
- ❏ friendship bracelets

❏ other _____

My favorite color is _____.

I think my best artwork this summer was _____

_____

_____

_____.

I like to learn about art from _____.

I went to an art museum this summer called ˉ

_____

_____.

My favorite artist is _____.

DRAMA

"When the curtain goes up, you will be onstage. Good luck."

. . . The curtain rose.

My heart beat fast in my chest. I looked in the audience. I saw everyone from my little-house family and everyone from my big-house family.

FROM #37 KAREN'S TUBA

If I were in a play I would like to be the:

❏ star   ❏ musician
❏ conductor   ❏ supporting actor
❏ narrator   ❏ costume designer
❏ light director   ❏ makeup artist
❏ other _____

If I could be the star of any show, the character I would like to play is _____

from _____.

I would like to learn these kinds of dances:

- ❑ ballet
- ❑ tap
- ❑ modern
- ❑ African
- ❑ other _____

- ❑ jazz
- ❑ cha-cha
- ❑ street
- ❑ circle

My favorite song from a show is _____.

An instrument that I like to play (or would like to learn how to play) is _____.

This summer my friends and I put on a play for

_____.

It was about _____

_____

_____.

I thought the play was _____.

I have seen _____ shows this summer.

My favorite show is _____.

SUMMER WEAR

Here is a good thing about summer: You do not have to wear too many clothes. In the summer I can get dressed in a flash. Underwear, shorts, shirt. If I am not going to leave my yard, those are the only clothes I have to put on. (If I am going to leave the yard, then I have to put on sandals, or maybe socks and sneakers.)

I can get dressed in about ten seconds.

FROM SUPER SPECIAL #4 KAREN, HANNIE, AND NANCY: THE THREE MUSKETEERS

The fastest I can get dressed is _____ seconds.

My favorite summer outfit is my _____.

My summer clothing (describe):

Favorite T-shirt _____

Favorite shorts _____

Favorite shoes _____

Favorite dress _____

Favorite hat _____

Other _____

My bathing suit is this color (or these colors):

_____.

My sunglasses look like this:
Draw a picture of your sunglasses here.

NATURE WALKS

"Hi, Bobby!" said Nancy and I.

"Want to go to the brook with me?" he asked.

There is a little brook not far from Bobby's house. I had almost forgotten about it. It is pretty boring in the wintertime. But now that summer was almost here, that brook would be full of minnows. And we would probably see dragonflies and water spiders and newts and maybe frogs.

"Yes!" I exclaimed.

FROM #50 KAREN'S LUCKY PENNY

On my nature walk I saw

❏ birds ❏ rocks

❏ trees ❏ a brook

❏ flowers ❏ animals

❏ butterflies ❏ mushrooms

Some other things I saw on the nature walk were:

_____

_____

_____.

I ☐ did ☐ did not carry a backpack.

I ☐ did ☐ did not get tired.

This is where I took my hike: _____.

The weather was _____.

I went on my nature walk with _____.

SECRET GARDENS

[Granny] showed me how to weed. She showed me how to use her gardening tools. And then she said, "Karen, would you like to be in charge of the garden while you are here?"

"Me?" I cried. "Really? You mean I can take care of the plants?"

"And pick the vegetables, too. We can have a fresh salad every night with dinner."

"A salad right out of my garden," I said. "Cool. Okay. I will take the job."

FROM SUPER SPECIAL #2 KAREN'S PLANE TRIP

I ☐ like ☐ don't like to garden.

This is what I (would) grow in my garden:

_____

_____

_____.

The vegetables from my garden that I like to eat are:

_____

_____.

I like to wear _____ when I garden.

I ☐ do ☐ do not like to wear gardening gloves when I garden.

I ☐ do ☐ do not like to get dirty when I garden.

I think taking care of a garden is
    ☐ easy   ☐ difficult
    ☐ sometimes easy, sometimes difficult

The thing that I like most about gardening is

_____

_____

_____.

FUN ON THE FARM

Suddenly Grandad said, "There it is, Karen!"
"What?"
"Our farm. It's straight ahead. See the silo? And the barn?"
They were way off in the distance. But I could see them. As we drove closer to the farm, I saw other things. I saw the tractor. I saw a field of cows. I saw some gardens. I saw a pigpen and a chicken coop.

FROM SUPER SPECIAL #2 KAREN'S PLANE TRIP

This summer I visited a farm called _____

_____

_____.

The people I met there were _____.

I saw these animals on the farm: _____

_____

_____.

This is what grew on the farm: _____

_____.

My favorite part of the farm was _____

_____.

Something I learned at the farm was _____

_____

_____.

A SUMMER CLUB

Hannie got a kitten. Now she and Amanda and I all have cats. I think we should start a club. The Kittycat Club.

FROM #4 KAREN'S KITTYCAT CLUB

The name of my club is _____.

These are the people in my club: _____

_____

_____.

My position in the club is _____.

We ☐ do ☐ do not have a clubhouse.

We meet: _____.

These are some of the things that my club does:

_____

_____

_____

_____.

SUMMER WISHES

"Hey!" I cried. "A lucky penny!" On the sidewalk in front of me lay a penny. It was shiny and brand-new. It was also heads up.

"Ooh, it is a lucky penny," said Nancy. "Put it in your pocket, Karen."

I did. I decided to keep it with me at all times.

FROM #50 KAREN'S LUCKY PENNY

I have a _____ as a good-luck charm.

This is how I got my good-luck charm: _____

_____

_____

_____.

I carry it with me

❏ all the time

❏ on special occasions

❏ sometimes

❏ when I'm feeling lucky

❏ when I'm feeling unlucky

❏ when I want to make a wish

❏ when I _____.

If I could make one wish for this summer, I would wish

for _____

_____.

The luckiest thing that happened to me this summer

was _____

_____

_____.

SUMMER STORIES

"Karen! Karen!" *Kristy was calling me from upstairs.*
"Coming!" *I answered. . . .*
Kristy was waiting in my room. I climbed into bed and hugged Moosie.
"Well," *said Kristy,* *"What story shall we read? The* Witch Next Door?"
The Witch Next Door *is my all-time favorite story.*

FROM #3 KAREN'S WORST DAY

My favorite book is _____

by _____ .

The funniest book I have ever read is _____

_____ .

The longest book I have ever read is _____
_____.

My favorite place to read is _____.

I like to read:
- ❏ fiction   ❏ biographies
- ❏ poetry   ❏ mysteries
- ❏ nonfiction   ❏ romance
- ❏ science fiction   ❏ short stories
- ❏ thrillers

Before the summer is over, I plan to finish
____ books.

I get most of my books from:
- ❏ the bookstore   ❏ the library
- ❏ friends   ❏ relatives
- ❏ other _____

These are some of the books I want to read: _____
_____
_____

Sometimes I like to have stories read to me. My favorite
reader is _____.

_____ told the scariest story
this summer.

STORY TELLERS

On Saturday, I woke up feeling excited. It was a very special day. It was not a holiday. It was the day the famous author was coming to town. This author does not write long, hard books for big people. She writes funny books for kids. Her name is Mary R. Sanderson. I love her books! And now I was going to have the chance to meet her.

FROM #20 KAREN'S CARNIVAL

My favorite author is _____.

If I could meet my favorite author this is what I would say to him or her: _____

_____

_____.

If I wrote a book it would be about _____

_____

_____.

I would title my book _____.

A summary reading chart:

Title	Author	Date started	Date finished	My opinion

NEWSPAPER AND MAGAZINES

*Wow! I was headline news: STONEYBROOK
ACADEMY STUDENT TO ENTER FAIRFIELD COUNTY
SPELLING BEE.*

*There was an article about the spelling bee inside.
And my picture was right next to it!*

*"Look at this! I'm in the newspaper!" I called to
everyone.*

FROM #11 KAREN'S PRIZE

I ❑ have ❑ have never been in a newspaper or a
magazine.

My favorite newspaper is _____.

My favorite magazine is _____.

I like reading these subjects or columns in newspapers
and magazines:

❑ health   ❑ nature
❑ current events   ❑ horoscopes
❑ movies   ❑ beauty

❑ new products   ❑ comics

❑ science   ❑ sports

❑ music   ❑ animals

❑ famous people

I like to read the newspaper while I am _____

_____

_____.

I like to read magazines while I am _____

_____

_____.

I have a subscription to _____.

SUMMER ROLLING

My skates are so, so cool. They are red. They are the lace-up kind. The wheels are yellow. . . .

I try to remember to be careful, but sometimes I forget. It is fun to go fast. It is fun to jump. When I go fast, I feel like I'm flying.

FROM #2 KAREN'S ROLLER SKATES

My roller skates or Rollerblades are this color:

_____

I think it is fun to _____ on my roller skates or Rollerblades.

These are the tricks I can do: _____

_____

_____

I ☐ can ☐ cannot skate backwards.

This is what I wear when I skate or blade: _____

_____

_____

For safety, I also wear:
- ❏ a helmet
- ❏ kneeguards
- ❏ wristguards
- ❏ elbow guards

The kind of bike I have is a _____.

I got my bike from _____.

I like to ride ____ slow ____ medium ____ fast.

The farthest I ever rode my bike was _____

_____.

SUMMER TUNES

"I better listen to the radio." I turned on my pink
sound box. The sound box is very cool. It is a radio and
a tape player. Plus, it has a microphone so I can pretend
I am a singer on the stage. Usually, I also pretend I have
a large audience.

FROM #34 KAREN'S SNOW DAY

The color radio I like to listen to is _____
_____.

My favorite radio station is _____.

The type of music I like to listen to most is _____
_____.

My favorite group is _____.

My favorite male singer is _____.

My favorite female singer is _____.

My favorite music video is _____.

My three favorite songs this summer are:

1. _____
   by _____
2. _____
   by _____
3. _____
   by _____

The best rainy day song is _____.

The best song to dance to is _____.

I like to listen to music when I'm _____
_____.

FOURTH OF JULY

As soon as it got dark, the fireworks started. They were gigundoly beautiful! First, a big red and orange star exploded in the sky. Just as it was disappearing, I heard a whistling in the air. Another rocket was flying up. It burst into blues and greens and fell like glitter all around.

"Yipee!" I shouted every time the sky lit up.

FROM #51 KAREN'S BIG TOP

I spent the Fourth of July with _____.

This is what we did: _____

_____

_____.

I ☐ did ☐ did not see fireworks.

We went to _____ to see the fireworks.

I shouted, "_____,"
as I saw the fireworks explode.

I thought the fireworks show was _____.

My favorite fireworks explosion was _____

_____.

For Fourth of July dinner I ate _____
_____
_____.

I ☐ did ☐ did not dress in red, white, and blue.

SOUNDS OF SUMMER

We left the cabin. We walked around the porch until we were facing the woods. Then we ran into the backyard. We stopped and listened. It was very quiet. I could hear water lapping and birds chirping, but those were quieter noises than Stoneybrook noises. No cars or horns or garbage trucks.

FROM SUPER SPECIAL #4 KAREN, HANNIE, AND NANCY: THE THREE MUSKETEERS

My favorite summer sound is _____.

These are other summer sounds that I like:

❑ fireworks   ❑ water

❑ waves   ❑ crickets

❑ motor boats   ❑ crackle of campfire

❑ rainfall   ❑ waterfall

I once heard a birdcall that sounded like _____
_____.

The funniest animal noise I have heard this summer came from a _____.

I heard it when I was _____.

I prefer ❑ loud noises ❑ soft sounds.

I ❑ do ❑ do not like the sound of thunder.

SUMMER PASTIMES

"Do you want to take Hyacynthia for a walk in my doll carriage?" I asked Nancy.

. . . "Okay," said Nancy.

. . . Hyacynthia was all dressed and ready to go. . . . We put her gently in the carriage. Then we covered her with a blanket and pushed her carefully out the door. . . .

We each took a side. Then we rolled our baby doll proudly down the street.

FROM #23 KAREN'S DOLL

I ☐ do ☐ do not collect dolls.

My favorite doll's name is _____.

In the summer I like to take my doll _____.

This summer my hobby is making _____

and / or collecting _____.

I started my hobby _____.

I usually spend ___ hours a week working on my hobby.

Some things I would like to add to my collection are

_____.

So far I have _____ (amount) in my collection.

I lke my hobby because _____

_____

_____.

My best friend's hobby is _____

_____

_____.

CARNIVALS, FAIRS, PARADES

At dinner, Seth said, "The carnival is in town. Who wants to go? We can go tonight."

"I do!" shrieked Andrew and I.

So Seth took us to the carnival. We brought Nancy along. We rode on the Ferris wheel. We walked through a spook house. (Andrew cried.) We looked at ourselves in wobbly mirrors. We ate cotton candy. We played games. (Andrew won a stuffed cow.) We had a gigundoly fun time.

FROM SUPER SPECIAL #4 KAREN, HANNIE, AND NANCY: THE THREE MUSKETEERS

I went to a carnival or fair called _____.

This is what I did there: _____

_____

_____.

My favorite game was _____.

I won a _____.

The best parade I saw this summer celebrated
_____.

The coolest thing I saw in the parade was _____
_____.

At the parade I also saw:

   ☐ clowns   ☐ baton twirlers

   ☐ bands   ☐ floats

   ☐ balloons   ☐ famous people

I ☐ have ☐ have never been in a parade.

AMUSEMENT PARKS

"I want to go to Funland."

"That would be so, so cool!" agreed Hannie.

Funland is an amusement park. It is brand-new. It just opened.

FROM #50 KAREN'S LUCKY PENNY

The amusement park I went to this summer was called

_____.

I went there with _____

_____.

It took us _____ hours to get there.

My favorite ride was _____.

I thought the scariest ride was _____
_____.

The ride I went on the most was _____
_____.

I went on a water ride called the _____.

After that ride I was:
- ☐ dry
- ☐ a little wet
- ☐ drenched

While I was there I ate:
- ☐ cotton candy
- ☐ popcorn
- ☐ hot dogs
- ☐ corndogs
- ☐ pretzels
- ☐ ice cream
- ☐ nachos with cheese
- ☐ other _____

SUMMER MONEY

"I still want to go skating," said Hannie.

I stretched my legs out in front of me. The sunshine felt good on them. But the porch stairs were uncomfortable. I wanted to go skating, too.

"Well, we can't," said Nancy. "We don't have skates. So that is that."

. . . "Maybe we could earn money to buy skates," I added.

FROM #20 KAREN'S CARNIVAL

This summer I earned money by _____.

I spent my money on _____.

I am saving my money for _____
_____.

If I had a lot of money to give to a charity, I would want to give it to _____.

If I won $100,000 this summer I would _____
_____
_____.

RAINY DAYS

Plink! Plunk! Plink! Plunk!

Raindrops were falling on the lid of the garbage can out in the yard. The noise was making me crabby. I am usually not a crabby person. I am usually a gigundoly happy person. . . .

Plink! Plunk! Plink! Plunk!

"I know what. I will call Nancy. We can have a rainy day tea party."

FROM #30 KAREN'S KITTENS

I ❑ like ❑ sometimes like ❑ dislike rainy days.

On rainy days I feel _____.

My favorite thing to do on a rainy day is _____
_____
_____.

A rainy day is a good time to learn how to do something.
(One rainy day, Granny taught Karen how to knit.) On a
rainy day I learned how to _____
_____.

When I have a friend over on a rainy day, we like to
_____
_____.

I think some good rainy day activities are:

❑ reading   ❑ watching TV
❑ talking on the phone   ❑ baking cookies
❑ drawing pictures   ❑ playing games
❑ playing cards   ❑ doing puzzles
❑ playing dress-up   ❑ making up my own
❑ practicing magic tricks   games
❑ other _____

Here's an idea I have for a great game: _____
_____.

SUMMER BUMMERS

"Now let me count up my bad things." I used my fingers to count.

". . . Fourteen bad things . . . . Fourteen!"

. . . *"Gosh,"* said Kristy, *"if there were a prize for bad days, you would win it, Karen."*

"I think," I said, *"that this is the first good thing that's happened to me today. I set a bad-day record!"*

FROM #3 KAREN'S WORST DAY

My worst day this summer was on _____.

This summer I got:

- ❏ poison ivy
- ❏ a sunburn
- ❏ a toothache
- ❏ an earache
- ❏ seasick
- ❏ a cut

❑ a bad haircut   ❑ a mosquito bite
❑ a bee sting   ❑ stitches
❑ scrapes and bruises   ❑ sniffles and sneezes
❑ a sore throat   ❑ a broken _____
❑ nothing   ❑ other _____

The absolute worst thing that happened to me this
summer was _____
_____.

I finally felt better when _____
_____
_____.

LOOKING BACK ON SUMMER

"You know what?" I said to Mommy as we stepped onto our porch. "This is our last night in Sea City. And we will eat our last dinner here. Everything that happens from now on will be the last."

FROM #52 KAREN'S MERMAID

The last thing I want to do before summer ends is

_____

_____.

I laughed the most when _____

_____

_____.

I'll never forget the time when _____

_____

_____.

The funniest / silliest thing that I did this summer was when I _____

_____

_____.

The scariest thing that happened to me this summer was

_____.

_____.

The bravest thing I did this summer was _____

_____.

The funniest joke I heard this summer was _____

_____

_____

_____.

The best thing that happened to me was _____

_____

_____.

This summer I was really happy when _____

_____

_____.

This summer I am really glad I learned _____

_____.

The sunniest day was on _____.

I saw the most stars on _____.

Before this summer I never knew _____.

The summer's best:

Playground _____

Park _____

Beach _____

Pool _____

Zoo _____

Museum _____

Party _____

Friend _____

Restaurant _____

Trip _____

Picnic _____

Sport _____

Ice cream _____

SUMMER'S END

Here is a picture of me at the end of summer.

Draw a picture or paste a photograph of yourself here.

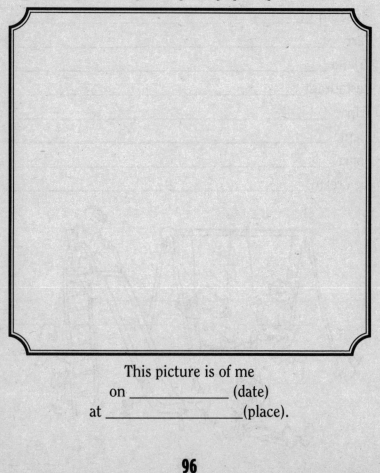

This picture is of me
on _____ (date)
at _____ (place).

SPECIAL DAYS

Special days to remember in
JUNE:

_____
_____
_____
_____
_____
_____
_____
_____

Special days to remember in
JULY:

_____

_____

_____

_____

_____

_____

_____

_____

Special days to remember in
AUGUST:

_____

_____

_____

_____

_____

_____

_____

_____

BACK TO SCHOOL

It was a September Saturday morning. September is one of my favorite months. When September comes, school starts.

FROM #53 KAREN'S SCHOOL BUS

My school starts on _____.

The name of the school I will be going to is

_____.

I will be in the ____ grade.

My teacher will be _____.

This is how I will get to school: _____.

My favorite back-to-school clothing item is _____

_____.

School supplies I got for this year are:

   ☑ a notebook   ☑ pencils   ☑ pens

   ☑ markers   ☑ books   ☑ paper

   ☑ a ruler   ☑ erasers   ☑ glue

   ☐ other _____

I plan to carry my books to school in _____.

Friends I haven't seen since school last year are

_____.

This year in school I will try to _____

_____.

I'm looking forward to school starting because

_____

_____

_____.

SUMMER MEMORIES

It was time to go home. Hannie and Nancy and I had bought our souvenirs.

FROM #50 KAREN'S LUCKY PENNY

Here is a great place to save souvenirs from summer. Paste down anything you wish — a photograph, a ticket stub, a leaf, or a ribbon you won — anything that will remind you of your special summer.

ADDRESSES OF SUMMER FRIENDS

"Look at that, Moosie!" I exclaimed. "I had to say good-bye to Amanda, but now I have her letter."

That is a good thing, I thought. Even when you have to say good-bye to someone, they can still be with you. You could have a letter, or pictures, or special memories.

FROM #19 KAREN'S GOOD-BYE

Fill in your friends' addresses and a special memory.

Name _____

Address _____

_____

Phone _____

Special memory _____

Name _____

Address _____

_____

Phone _____

Special memory _____

Name _____

Address _____

_____

Phone _____

Special memory _____

Name __Maddy_____

Address _____

_____

Phone _____

Special memory:_____

Name _____

Address _____

_____

Phone _____

Special memory:_____

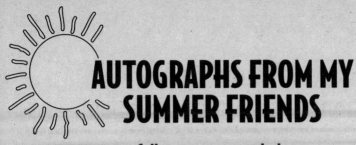

AUTOGRAPHS FROM MY SUMMER FRIENDS

Collect your autographs here.

Karen Brewer and her
friends are jumping for joy!

All-new!

BABY·SITTERS
Little Sister®

Comes with a colorful jump rope!

Jump Rope Rhymes Pack

You'll love singing and jumping along
with the rhymes, games, and lots more
inside this new Little Sister pack!
Learn all the alphabet rhymes, classic
rhymes and Double Dutch rhymes from the
book—then practice your fancy footwork
with the jump rope that's included.
It's easy to have a ton of fun with your
friends, just like Karen does!

Coming in July.

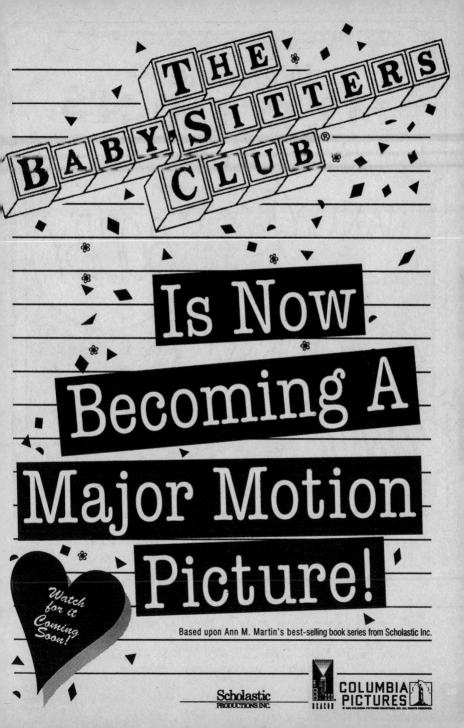

Meet some new friends in a brand-new
series just right for _you_.
Starring **Baby-sitters Little Sister**
Karen Brewer...
and everyone else in the second grade.

Look for THE KIDS IN MS. COLMAN'S CLASS #1: TEACHERS PET.
Coming to your bookstore in September.

888888888LITTLE 🍎 APPLE®888888888

BABY·SITTERS
Little Sister™
by Ann M. Martin, author of *The Baby-sitters Club*®

❑ MQ44300-3	#1	Karen's Witch	$2.95
❑ MQ44259-7	#2	Karen's Roller Skates	$2.95
❑ MQ44299-7	#3	Karen's Worst Day	$2.95
❑ MQ44264-3	#4	Karen's Kittycat Club	$2.95
❑ MQ44258-9	#5	Karen's School Picture	$2.95
❑ MQ44298-8	#6	Karen's Little Sister	$2.95
❑ MQ44257-0	#7	Karen's Birthday	$2.95
❑ MQ42670-2	#8	Karen's Haircut	$2.95
❑ MQ43652-X	#9	Karen's Sleepover	$2.95
❑ MQ43651-1	#10	Karen's Grandmothers	$2.95
❑ MQ43650-3	#11	Karen's Prize	$2.95
❑ MQ43649-X	#12	Karen's Ghost	$2.95
❑ MQ43648-1	#13	Karen's Surprise	$2.75
❑ MQ43646-5	#14	Karen's New Year	$2.75
❑ MQ43645-7	#15	Karen's in Love	$2.75
❑ MQ43644-9	#16	Karen's Goldfish	$2.75
❑ MQ43643-0	#17	Karen's Brothers	$2.75
❑ MQ43642-2	#18	Karen's Home-Run	$2.75
❑ MQ43641-4	#19	Karen's Good-Bye	$2.95
❑ MQ44823-4	#20	Karen's Carnival	$2.75
❑ MQ44824-2	#21	Karen's New Teacher	$2.95
❑ MQ44833-1	#22	Karen's Little Witch	$2.95
❑ MQ44832-3	#23	Karen's Doll	$2.95
❑ MQ44859-5	#24	Karen's School Trip	$2.95
❑ MQ44831-5	#25	Karen's Pen Pal	$2.95
❑ MQ44830-7	#26	Karen's Ducklings	$2.75
❑ MQ44829-3	#27	Karen's Big Joke	$2.95
❑ MQ44828-5	#28	Karen's Tea Party	$2.95

More Titles... ➡

888888888888888888888888888888

The Baby-sitters Little Sister titles continued...

❑ MQ44825-0	#29	Karen's Cartwheel	$2.75
❑ MQ45645-8	#30	Karen's Kittens	$2.75
❑ MQ45646-6	#31	Karen's Bully	$2.95
❑ MQ45617-1	#32	Karen's Pumpkin Patch	$2.95
❑ MQ45648-2	#33	Karen's Secret	$2.95
❑ MQ45650-4	#34	Karen's Snow Day	$2.95
❑ MQ45652-0	#35	Karen's Doll Hospital	$2.95
❑ MQ45651-2	#36	Karen's New Friend	$2.95
❑ MQ45653-9	#37	Karen's Tuba	$2.95
❑ MQ45655-5	#38	Karen's Big Lie	$2.95
❑ MQ45654-7	#39	Karen's Wedding	$2.95
❑ MQ47040-X	#40	Karen's Newspaper	$2.95
❑ MQ47041-8	#41	Karen's School	$2.95
❑ MQ47042-6	#42	Karen's Pizza Party	$2.95
❑ MQ46912-6	#43	Karen's Toothache	$2.95
❑ MQ47043-4	#44	Karen's Big Weekend	$2.95
❑ MQ47044-2	#45	Karen's Twin	$2.95
❑ MQ47045-0	#46	Karen's Baby-sitter	$2.95
❑ MQ43647-3		Karen's Wish Super Special #1	$2.95
❑ MQ44834-X		Karen's Plane Trip Super Special #2	$3.25
❑ MQ44827-7		Karen's Mystery Super Special #3	$2.95
❑ MQ45644-X		Karen's Three Musketeers Super Special #4	$2.95
❑ MQ45649-0		Karen's Baby Super Special #5	$3.25
❑ MQ46911-8		Karen's Campout Super Special #6	$3.25

Available wherever you buy books, or use this order form.